RABASH

Rabash

Story and Paintings by CLAUDINE

Hurwitz

THE MACMILLAN COMPANY, NEW YORK

Library of Congress catalog card number: 65-20491

The Macmillan Company, New York
Collier–Macmillan Canada, Ltd., Toronto, Ontario

Designed by Mina Baylis

Printed in the United States of America

First Printing

For *ALEXANDRA*

THERE once was, in the kingdom of Persia, a little prince named Kasim.

One night when it was time for him to go to bed, a great storm swept down from the mountains. The wind blew and the rain fell in torrents.

Prince Kasim was frightened. He ran to see his father, King Rustam. "Papa," he cried, "the storm is trying to get into my room!"

The wind raised its voice just then.

King Rustam patted his son's head. "Come, I will read you a story," he said. "When I am finished, the storm will be gone."

The king wrapped his robes about him. "Now, which story shall it be?"

"The story of Rabash!" cried Prince Kasim.

King Rustam clapped his hands, and a courtier hurried to bring the prince's favorite storybook.

The king straightened his crown, opened the book, and began to read: "Once there was a little blue horse named Rabash. He longed to visit the forest, but he lived in the city, behind closed gates. . . ."

Prince Kasim leaned forward to look at Rabash. He put out one finger to pat the little blue horse.

Suddenly a strange thing happened. The little horse moved! He shivered and shook himself in the picture.

"Papa!" Kasim cried. "Rabash moved!"

"It was the wind rustling the pages . . ." the king started to say. But a giant clap of thunder cut off his words.

The little horse reared up on his hind legs and pawed the air with his black hooves. Then he leaped right out of the book and sped down the long corridor.

"Rabash!" the prince cried, running after him.

"Rabash!" the king cried, running after the prince.

"Rabash!" cried the courtiers, running after the king.

And the cook from the kitchen came running last of all. "Rabash!" he shouted. "Wait! Come back! Come back!"

But the little horse did not stop. He raced on, his black mane flying, his black hooves clip-clopping on the cobblestones.

"Stop him!" the king commanded.

A guard dashed forward to slam the gate shut, but he was too late. The little horse galloped off into the night.

"Oh, Rabash!" the prince cried. "Come back, please come back!"

The little horse did not hear him. He galloped on through the rain, his eyes bright with excitement. He splashed happily through the puddles. He felt the coolness of the rain pattering on his nose and knees.

Rabash ran and ran. The roar of the thunder turned to a chuckle. The howl of the wind became a gay song.

In the morning, the sun came out and shone down on Rabash. He found himself in the forest.

He sniffed the fresh air. He nibbled the green grass. He drank from a sparkling pool. He was so happy that he whinnied, and that made him laugh.

"Hello," cried a red bird with a great long tail. "Who are you?"

Rabash looked up, startled. "I am Rabash," he said. "I have come to live in the forest."

"Well, then, I will lead you to the others," the red bird said. And he sailed away through the trees.

Rabash trotted happily after him. His eyes grew wider and wider at all the wonders he saw.

"Look!" called the red bird finally. "See what I found for you!"

Rabash peered past a bush, and there, grazing in the glen, were six gleaming wild horses.

When they noticed Rabash, they were surprised. None of them had seen a blue horse before.

"What do you want, little blue horse?" they asked.

"I want to live in the forest—with you," said Rabash timidly.

"For a visit?" asked the wild horses. "Or forever?"

"Oh, forever," Rabash replied.

The red bird began to sing. The flowers began to nod. The cypress trees rustled their branches. And Rabash pranced and danced in the glen with his new friends.

That same morning, Prince Kasim was very sad. He missed Rabash, and he was afraid for him.

King Rustam called in his royal guards, saying, "Search throughout my kingdom. Look in all the closets, look in all the cupboards, look in all the courtyards—Rabash must be found!"

The king's men set off in all directions. They poked in all the closets. They peeked in all the cupboards. They looked in all the courtyards. And they shook out all the rugs in Persia seeking for the little horse.

Finally they came to the forest. There, in the moonlight, Rabash slept beside his friends.

It was very quiet. The larks and the quail, the parrots and the partridges were sleeping. The red bird was sleeping, too.

No one saw the guards tiptoe into the shadows. Then the commander held up his hand. "There he is," he whispered to his men. "His eyes are closed. Good."

He raised his sword high into the air and said a magic word he had learned in Baghdad. A silk bridle appeared from nowhere. It fell softly over the little horse's head.

Rabash woke with a start. His legs were shaking.

"We will not hurt you," the commander

said. "But we must take you back to the palace to Prince Kasim. Come along, now."

He led Rabash out of the shadows to his men. They jumped onto their horses, wheeled them about, and, with Rabash between them, set off for the palace.

The red bird woke and cried out.

Rabash heard him, but it was too late. Two big, shiny tears slipped out of his eyes. "Good-by, forest," he thought as he was whisked away.

In no time at all, the warriors arrived at the palace gates. Trumpets sounded and bugles blew.

Prince Kasim came running downstairs, calling, "Rabash! Rabash, you have come home!"

He threw his arms around the little horse and hugged him tight. Rabash had never been hugged before.

King Rustam called for a celebration.

In the garden, a beautiful pavilion was built, and Prince Kasim brushed the horse's coat till it shone.

People came from far and near.

Viziers came dressed in scarlet and silver.

Potentates in purple robes came riding on camels.

Agas came wearing crowns that looked like cages of yellow canaries.

Everyone came to marvel at Rabash.

The king beamed. "This little horse is the pride of my kingdom," he proclaimed.

"He is going to stay with us always!" Prince Kasim cried.

Then a great feast of almonds and oranges and brown-sugar candy appeared, and for Rabash there was a bucketful of oats and a big red apple.

Every day after that, Prince Kasim and Rabash played in the garden. The little horse learned many tricks. He learned how to leap over pools and fountains. He learned how to bow low so that Kasim could climb up on his back.

"Come, Rabash!" Kasim would shout. "Jump the high hedges!" Together they would gallop along the garden paths, through the courtyards, under the arches, while the guards applauded and the king smiled.

But sometimes Rabash would gaze out through the gate at the green forest, and his eyes would grow sad. Then Prince Kasim would slide down from his back, and, stroking his mane, would stand beside him, looking through the bars of the gate.

"What is the forest like?" wondered Kasim, who had never been beyond the palace garden himself.

One night when the prince was in bed, he heard Rabash whinnying under his window. For a minute the prince lay quite still. Then he stole out of bed and, quiet as a hummingbird, went down the stairs and crept into the garden.

Rabash was at the gate, pawing the ground.

Prince Kasim patted the horse's neck. Then he said out loud, "What is the forest like, Rabash? Does anybody live there?"

Then the prince drew a deep breath. "Rabash, we could run away to the forest! No one will see us. Everyone is sleeping."

The horse's heart beat faster.

"Yes, Rabash," said Kasim, "let's go!" Then he leaped onto his back, and together they raced along the path and sailed over the palace gates. Together they ran and ran, deep into the forest.

"Oh, Rabash," Prince Kasim said, jumping down from the horse's back, "how beautiful the forest is! The trees are as tall as palace towers. The moss is as soft as palace rugs."

Rabash tossed his mane and pranced with joy. But out of the corner of his eye he watched for shadows that moved, shadows that could be the king's royal guards.

Suddenly Kasim heard the whistle of wings. It was the red bird.

"Rabash is back! Rabash is back!" he sang, swooping onto a branch just over Kasim's head. "We thought you were stolen forever."

"We have run away from the palace," Rabash said. "This is Prince Kasim, who has never seen the forest before." Then Rabash told the red bird how he was taken away by King Rustam's warriors and given oats and apples and honored at a great celebration.

Kasim and Rabash stood together looking up at the red bird. The moonlight braided itself in the bird's long tail. The forest seemed alive with tiny sounds and stirrings.

"I like the forest," said Kasim.

The red bird nodded and said to Rabash, "Well, then, the prince is welcome here. I shall go and tell the others." And with that, he glided away into the darkness.

Just then, out of nowhere, came a crashing, growling lion! His eyes were yellow and his claws were sharp.

Rabash saw the lion first and whinnied to warn the prince.

"Watch out, Rabash!" Kasim cried. The little boy jumped up onto the branch overhead, not a moment before the lion leaped forward.

Rabash spun to one side. With an angry growl, the lion snapped his jaws open. The little horse reared up, and before the lion could swing around, he brought his black hooves down on the lion's back. The beast tumbled to the ground, roaring a roar that was heard in the faraway mountains.

The prince was frightened. He whispered, "Oh, Rabash, be careful."

Then the lion was up again, growling.

Kasim's tree trembled. The air quivered. A thundering was everywhere, like a storm sweeping through the forest.

Rabash tossed his head and twitched his ears.

All of a sudden, on all sides, the wild horses appeared. The forest was full of them, running, galloping, stamping the ground.

The lion was surrounded. Then, with one great, snarling leap, he sprang upon the little blue horse. Rabash fell, and across his head Kasim saw a streak of bright red.

"Rabash!" the prince cried out. He hid his face in his hands.

With a terrible roar, the lion turned and dashed away among the trees.

The wild horses gathered around Rabash, who looked like a blue flower lying on the moss. On his head, where the lion's claws had reached out, sat an old friend. Kasim could not believe his eyes. It was the red bird!

"Rabash!" Kasim said in wonder. "Rabash, you are safe!" He almost fell right out of the tree. In a moment, the prince was kneeling beside his friend. Rabash nuzzled the little boy's hand. And the red bird started to sing.

Just then there was a clatter. King Rustam and his warriors on horseback burst into the forest.

"Papa!" Kasim shouted. "Rabash is safe after all! There was a lion here with yellow eyes and sharp claws. I thought Rabash was hurt, but it was really the red bird."

King Rustam hugged his son and listened to his story. "Rabash is a very brave horse," the king said finally. "He shall have a reward. He shall have a bridle of gold and reins of silk and a saddle of the finest leather."

"Papa," Kasim interrupted, "Rabash should have a better reward than that, for he is the bravest horse in all the world. He should have the forest as a reward. He loves the forest—and so do I."

His father answered, "I am the king, it is true. But even I cannot move the forest into the palace garden."

"No, Papa," said the prince. "The forest will stay where it is, and Rabash will stay in it." Kasim looked at the little horse standing proudly among the others. He thought of the times they had spent together, when Rabash was learning to be alive. He turned to his father and said, "Rabash belongs here, where he is free."

1433027

"You will miss him," King Rustam replied.

"I know," said the prince, feeling sad and happy at the same time. "I shall come to visit him whenever I can."

The sun was in the sky again. The wild horses trotted a little distance away as Kasim gave Rabash a bit of brown sugar he had saved for just such a breakfast in the forest.

No one knows what passed between them that morning, but everyone in Persia knows that on stormy nights, when the wind howls and the rain blows, a boy and a horse are heard galloping happily among the trees in the forest they love.

1833